TAKE SNOW CHANCES

A HOLIDAY COZY MYSTERY

PATTI BENNING

SUMMER PRESCOTT BOOKS PUBLISHING

Copyright 2024 Summer Prescott Books

All Rights Reserved. No part of this publication nor any of the information herein may be quoted from, nor reproduced, in any form, including but not limited to: printing, scanning, photocopying, or any other printed, digital, or audio formats, without prior express written consent of the copyright holder.

**This book is a work of fiction. Any similarities to persons, living or dead, places of business, or situations past or present, is completely unintentional.

CHAPTER ONE

Nola Shepherd gazed into the snow as it swirled in front of the headlights. It was beautiful and mesmerizing, and it made her glad she wasn't the one driving.

"It looks like the turn is only a quarter of a mile away," she told Henry. "You might want to slow down a little more. I'm not sure if we'll be able to see the sign at all in this."

"Thank goodness we're almost there," he said, easing the brake pedal down. The storm had hit nearly an hour ago, and the road was almost nonexistent. "We should have waited until tomorrow to come out here."

"To be fair to my parents, the storm wasn't supposed to start for another two hours," she said. She looked out the side window. Everything was just *white.* She couldn't even see the trees on the other side of the road. "But yeah… this is bad."

With it being the first year that both of her parents were retired, they had wanted to do something special for the holidays. A week-long stay at Rocky Haven Mountain Retreat over Christmas for the entire family was the end result, which had sounded perfectly nice until the weather reports started warning of a blizzard. With two cabins and an all-inclusive stay for Nola, her husband Henry, both her parents, and her younger sister all paid for, canceling the trip hadn't been in the books.

Nola was just glad they were nearly there without anyone getting stuck in a snow drift. She turned down the radio, which was playing holiday music on repeat, but then turned it up again when the song ended and the broadcaster came on, a new, serious tone in his voice.

"Good evening, ladies and gentlemen. I just got a report about a robbery of an armored truck, leaving behind one victim. The suspect absconded with a significant sum of money. Details are still coming in,

but if any of our local listeners has any tips for the police, please call the following number..."

"Huh," Henry said as the broadcaster listed off the number. "Whoever did *that* sure isn't in the holiday spirit."

"None of this is getting me into the holiday spirit," she grumbled. "I think I'm voting to stay home next year."

Henry hit the blinker and slowed the SUV to a crawl while they searched for the retreat's entrance. A gap between two large pines, a sign nearly buried in a snowdrift, and an expanse of slightly shallower snow was the only hint that they had found it. Henry took the turn, and the SUV faithfully plowed through the powdery snow. Behind them, the vehicle her parents and her sister were carpooling in followed them.

The barely visible drive wound its way partway up the mountainside. It was slow going, but soon enough, the resort's lights came into view and she breathed a sigh of relief. At least none of them were going to spend Christmas stranded in the snow, though she wasn't sure how many of the retreat's promised activities would be available in a snowstorm. Being together was the important part.

If the parking lot had any lines delegating the spots, they were buried under the snow, so Henry made an educated guess as he parked in front of the building that looked like it was the retreat's lobby. It had lights on, at least, and there were other vehicles in the lot, which was a promising sign. There were supposed to be cabins nearby, but if there were, they were lost in the storm.

Henry kept the SUV running and the two of them huddled in the warm air until her parents had parked. Nola exchanged a look with her husband.

"If I freeze to death out there, just know that I love you and I'm sorry I didn't convince them to spend Christmas in the Bahamas."

"I love you too," he said seriously. "And I forgive you."

They grinned at each other, then reached to open their doors. The wind hit Nola with all the force of a rapidly moving wall, and she quickly slipped out of the vehicle and slammed the door shut behind her to keep the snow from blowing in and melting on the leather seats.

"What do you think?" her dad asked, nearly shouting over the wind. "Looks promising, doesn't it?"

"It mostly looks like a lot of snow," Nola called back. "Are you sure this is the right place?"

"It'd better be. I think your mom just might murder me if I told her we had to keep driving. Let's head in."

The five of them – herself, Henry, her father, her mother, and her sister – all headed toward the building with the lights on. They had to shuffle through the snow and make their best guess at where the path up to the entrance was. Thankfully, there was a sign under the overhang at the front welcoming them to Rocky Haven Mountain Retreat, which meant that at the very least, they were in the right place and wouldn't have to try to drive further up the mountain in the storm. Nola's father pulled the door open and held it for the rest of them as they trooped inside.

The interior was rustic, but a sort of modern, carefully designed rustic that reminded her of the ski lodge she had gone to for her spring break back in college. There was a huge, real Christmas tree in the corner, richly decorated, though the lights were currently unplugged. It was blessedly warm inside, especially once her father shut the heavy door behind them.

It was also completely empty, except for her family.

Nola trailed behind her father as he approached the counter, mostly to keep away from her mother, who was carefully wiping the snow off of her sister's coat. She could hear her sister complaining in the background.

There was a bell to ring for service, but no one came when her father made it chime. He raised his voice. "Hello? Is anyone here?"

The only answer was the sound of her sister yelping as their mother knocked some snow down the neck of her coat. Nola glanced at her father.

"Did you get any emails from them?" she asked. "Maybe they canceled the reservation because of the storm. Or maybe the staff went home early – tomorrow is Christmas Eve, after all."

"Let me check," he said, taking out his phone. She saw him look at the screen and frown, then look around the room. There was a laminated sheet of paper with the WiFi password on it taped to the counter, and she watched as he typed the password into his phone. Pulling her own phone out of her pocket, she realized that she didn't have any service up here.

At least this place has WiFi, she thought. *Though if the power goes out, we'll lose that too.*

She felt a chill at the thought of being stuck up here with no way to call out, but before she could give voice to her worries, her father made a relieved noise.

"They did send me an email. It says that if we get here past the check-in time, we can find our welcome packet behind the desk." He glanced at the clock on the wall. "Well, we aren't late, but maybe they had to go out and batten down the hatches for the storm. Let me just check…"

He stepped around the counter and glanced at his phone again as he crouched down and opened a drawer. He withdrew a large manila envelope with an exclamation of success.

"Here it is! The Shepherd Family. That's us. Right, let's look through this."

There was a nice sitting area, with some cozy, plush armchairs near a large fireplace – currently empty – and a large, square coffee table. They all sat down.

Her father opened the packet and shook it out over the table. Two keys fell out, along with a few papers.

"All right, we've got our cabin numbers – looks like they'll be right next to each other, that's good – oh, and here's a map."

"A map," her mother broke in. "How big is this place, Liam? We can't go hiking through the snow looking for some cabin in the middle of nowhere."

"The cabins aren't far," he said. "Just outside the door, really. They're arranged in a semi-circle around the parking area. They shouldn't be hard to find at all. I guess this is it; there aren't any other check-in instructions. What do you say we find our cabins and get unpacked?"

"Back out into the cold. Yay," Nola said dryly. Henry put an arm around her shoulder, giving her a brief hug. She sighed and forced herself to relax.

She was happy to be here with her family, she really was, it was just that she would have rather spent Christmas at her parents' home instead of making a multi-hour drive to a mountain in a snowstorm.

They braved the cold, and huddled around the map that Nola's father gripped tightly as they tried to figure out where the cabins were. Henry was the one who squinted into the snow and said, "I think they're that way."

They kept close together as they waded through the snow. She was glad the main building had its lights on, since it would make it harder to lose it in the storm. Before too long, a few shadowy forms came into view through the blowing snow, revealing themselves to be a line of cabins. When they hunted down the ones with the correct numbers on them, Nola's father handed her a key, and she and Henry hurried up to their door to unlock it. Nola pushed her way into the cozy little cabin with relief. After turning on the lights and looking around, she stuck her head back outside to see that her mother, father, and sister had managed to get into theirs.

"Well, at least we know we're not going to freeze out here," she said. "Though bringing all of our luggage inside isn't going to be fun."

"You stay in here and get the place warmed up," Henry told her. "I'll move the SUV closer, and bring our stuff in."

"Are you sure?"

He grinned. "Yes. I still feel like your dad doesn't think I'm good enough for you. I can't ignore a chance to show him what a doting husband I am."

"Well, fair warning – one of my bags might be a little heavy. I brought a lot of books."

He chuckled and gave her a quick kiss before stepping back out into the snow. Nola turned around to explore the cabin further. There was a fireplace, with wood stacked beside it, but she didn't want to mess with that just yet. She found the thermostat tucked between a bookshelf and the corner of the living room and turned the heat up from its minimum setting. A moment later, the furnace kicked to life, and she huddled in front of the vent, glad for the warm air.

The sound of voices outside brought her back over to the front door, and she peeked out. Henry had moved the car to a spot right in front of the cabin, and she could see that her father had done the same. Three other cabins had vehicles parked in front of them. The one at the end of the row to her left was the closest – a silver SUV was parked out front, but the cabin's windows were dark. She hoped whoever was renting it hadn't gotten lost in the storm.

The sight of Henry struggling to bring all of their luggage in with one trip made her feel bad, so she pulled her coat back on and went outside to help him. Her parents were still unloading their own vehicle, but her sister must have already brought all of her own things in – Nola could see her standing at the door to her parents' cabin, and she waved when she saw Nola looking at her. Nola waved back. She really wanted to spend some quality time with Ashley on this trip. She felt like she had barely seen her younger sister since last summer. Ashley was in the middle of her senior year at college, and had barely had time to meet for lunch every now and again. It was a miracle she had agreed to come on this trip in the first place.

"Well, we're here," her father shouted over the wind. "Let's get settled. We'll meet up later for dinner."

"We'll see you in a bit, Dad," Nola said. She grabbed the handles of two suitcases and pulled. Henry hefted her duffel bag full of books and gave an exaggerated wince before grabbing the other suitcase.

"Thanks again for setting this trip up, Liam," Henry called out to her father as he shouldered the bag. Then he turned to her, faking a stumble under the heavy weight. "I'm pretty sure you packed rocks instead of books in this one."

She snorted, and together they started heaving their luggage toward the door of their cabin.

CHAPTER TWO

"Nope, they're not under here either."

Nola shut the kitchen cabinets and turned around, looking around the small cabin with her hands on her hips. It was an open floor plan, with the living room and the kitchen sharing the same space. There was one bathroom and a bedroom, and not much room left over for anything else.

It was cozy, and perfectly comfortable for their stay, but it was lacking something very important. Towels. The only linens in the entire place seemed to be the spread on the bed and one folded blanket over the arm of the couch. There were no bath towels, no hand towels, not even any washcloths or rags. She desperately wanted to take a bath to recover from the cold,

cold weather, but she did not want to have to drip all over the place until the air dried her off.

"Do you want me to see if your parents have any?" Henry called from the bedroom, where he was desperately checking every nook and cranny for the towels.

"No, I'll go," she said. "You said you'd put that frozen pie in the oven, remember? My mom's making dinner, but we still have to bring *something*."

"All right." He stepped out of the bedroom. "I'll get started on that. Try not to get lost out there. Finding each other in a snowstorm sounds romantic, but I think it would probably just be cold."

"If I get lost between our cabin and my parents', which is roughly ten steps away, I probably deserve it," she said. She rose onto her tiptoes to kiss him. "But it's very sweet to know that you would come looking for me."

He grinned. "I wouldn't even make fun of you for getting lost in ten steps. That's how much I love you."

She was smiling as she put her boots and coat on, taking care to tuck her gloves into her sleeves and pull her hood up. She probably looked like an overstuffed grape in her wine-red coat, but she didn't care. She just wanted to be warm.

If anything, the storm had gotten worse while they were in the cabin. She shuffled out of the doorway, making sure to shut the door firmly behind her, and turned toward her parents' cabin. As she made her way through the snow, she tried to keep her spirits up. She knew her dad would be disappointed if the storm lasted their entire trip. Part of the draw of this place for him was all of the outdoor activities it offered. It would be hard to go skiing or snowshoeing if they couldn't see ten feet in front of them.

Once she reached the other cabin, she knocked on the door, then let herself in without waiting for a response. "Hey, do you guys have any extra towels?"

Her father looked up from where he had been building a fire in the fire place. "No, we don't. I told your mother and sister I would go get some from the lobby once I get this going. A fire seems like just the thing on a stormy night like tonight."

She sighed. "We're missing our towels too. I might as well go to the lobby since I'm already in my outdoor gear. I'll bring towels back for you guys too."

"Thanks, sweetie!" her mother called from the bedroom. Her sister called out too, asking for extra pillows. Nola wasn't sure about the logistics of carrying a bunch of linens and pillows back to the cabins through a storm, but she supposed she would have to figure it out.

Back outside, she hesitated, wondering if she should go in and get the car keys from Henry, but the lobby building wasn't far. She could see the lights even through the blowing snow, and it would probably take her longer to explain everything to Henry, get the windshield cleaned off, and get in and out of the car than it would to just walk over.

Hunching her shoulders against the wind, she set off, keeping her eyes on the lights in front of her. She was so focused on her destination that she almost didn't notice the shadowy figure that was walking through the parking lot from another cabin.

She paused, squinted to make sure she wasn't seeing things, then waved. "Hey!" she called out, figuring ignoring the other person would be more awkward.

The other figure jumped, which made her think they hadn't seen her until she spoke.

"Hello." It was a woman's voice. She shuffled closer, a featureless blob of blue in her plush coat. "Are you staying here too?" She had to almost shout to be heard over the storm.

"Yeah, we just got here. You heading toward the lobby?"

The other woman nodded, and they started walking again. Nola reached the door to the lobby first and held it open while the stranger went through. It was a relief to be in a shelter again, and she pulled her hood back with a sigh. The lobby was still empty, which wasn't promising. Maybe the linens closet was labeled, and she could just help herself.

The other woman pulled her hood back too, revealing long, dyed, dark red hair. "You chose a bad night to come here."

Nola made a face. "Trust me, I know. We left before the storm started, though. It wasn't supposed to hit for another few hours. How long have you been here? I'm Nola, by the way."

"I got here earlier today, while it was still clear," the woman said. She shook Nola's hand briefly. "Victoria."

"Nice to meet you. Were you out of towels too?"

Victoria gave her an odd look. "No. I need to pick up a toothbrush and toothpaste. The owner told me they sell them at the counter."

"Oh. Well, hopefully we can find someone to help us."

She moved over to the counter, ringing the service bell. For some reason, she always felt rude when she did that, even though that was why the bell was there.

This time, there was a response. A middle-aged woman with short hair and a light pink uniform stepped out of a room down the hall, pushing a cart full of cleaning supplies ahead of her. She abandoned the cart to come over to the counter. There was a name tag on her shirt that read *Anna*.

"How can I help you ladies?"

She gestured for Victoria to go first, and waited as the other woman exchanged cash for a toothbrush and a travel-sized tube of toothpaste. Then it was her turn.

"My parents and I are staying in cabins eight and nine, and both cabins seem to be missing towels and washcloths. Do you have some I could bring back? Oh, and extra pillows too."

The woman nodded brusquely. "Yes, ma'am. Sorry about the inconvenience. The storm hit sooner than expected, and it sidetracked me before I could finish preparing the cabins for you. I'll go fetch what you need, you just wait here."

Anna moved out from behind the counter. Victoria was still in the lobby, but she seemed to be focused on reading a pamphlet about the activities the resort offered, so Nola didn't strike up another conversation. She waited, watching as Anna bustled down the hall and pulled open a door opposite the one she had come out of before.

A scream filled the air. Nola jumped, and she saw Victoria drop the pamphlet out of the corner of her eye. Down the hall, Anna backpedaled out of the room, staring through the door with a horrified expression on her face.

"What happened?" Nola asked, beginning to move toward her.

In response, Anna just lifted a finger and silently pointed. Nola jogged the last few feet down the hall and looked in through an open door.

The sight inside hit her almost like a physical thing. A man was lying on the floor of what seemed to be a laundry room, the white tiles around him smeared red with his blood.

Nola had never seen a corpse before, but there was no doubt in her mind this man was very, very dead.

CHAPTER THREE

"What's going on?"

The question came from Victoria, who had joined them in the hall without Nola realizing it. She turned away from the gruesome sight in the laundry room and took in Anna's horrified expression and Victoria's pale, confused face.

She stepped aside and let Victoria look into the room, not sure if she could manage an explanation. Victoria took one look and winced before pulling the door shut.

"D-do you think he had a heart attack or something?" she whispered.

"Did you see all the *blood?*" Anna squeaked. "That wasn't a heart attack!"

"Guys, guys, we need to call the police," Nola said. "I mean, it's going to take them a while to get up here in the storm, isn't it? And it's just going to get worse the longer we wait..."

She wished suddenly and vehemently that she had asked Henry or one of her family to come with her to pick up the towels. She had never, not in her wildest dreams, thought she would stumble upon something like this. At least she wasn't *completely* alone. The two women might be strangers, but it would be worse if she was the only one in here with the dead body.

Anna seemed to snap out of her shock a little. She nodded and took a deep breath. "You're right. We should–"

Her mouth snapped shut as the door to the lobby opened. All three of them turned and looked down the hall to watch as a bundled-up figure came into the building. Nola's heart leapt, then sank immediately when she realized this wasn't Henry coming to look for her – it was a woman she had never seen before.

She pulled down her hood, revealing long brown hair that was just starting to grey, and took one look at the empty space behind the front desk before calling out, "Frank!"

Beside Nola, Anna twitched violently and looked toward the shut laundry room door. Nola surmised that Frank was the dead man.

When there was no answer, the woman glanced around, and finally saw the three of them. They must have looked odd, standing grouped together and staring at her. Nola wasn't sure what expression was on her face, but she was sure it wasn't pretty, and the other women didn't look any better.

The new woman blinked at them, and a flicker of unease crossed her face before she gathered herself.

"Anna! Where's Frank? Robert *still* isn't back. He needs to get in that truck of his and head into town. If something happened to my husband because of his ridiculous insistence–"

"Mrs. Russell." Anna paused, as if trying to figure out what to say before she bulldozed ahead. "Frank's dead."

The words seemed to linger in the silent lobby as Mrs. Russell's jaw worked itself. She seemed confused at first, as if she had misheard, and slowly her expression twisted into one of trepidation.

"What are you talking about?"

Silently, Anna gestured for her to approach them. Mrs. Russell moved down the hall, her steps more and more hesitant as she drew closer and closer.

When she reached them, Victoria frowned, then pushed the door open. Mrs. Russell peered inside, then quickly withdrew, slapping a hand over her mouth, her eyes wide.

Victoria shut the door briskly. Mrs. Russell looked between the three of them, her expression horrified. Slowly, she removed the hand from her mouth.

"What did you do?"

Nola frowned. "We didn't *do* anything. We just found him like that."

"Did you even check to see if he was alive?"

Now, Nola hesitated. They hadn't, but... he looked pretty dead.

"He's dead," Anna confirmed, her tone snappish. "It looked like someone stabbed him."

Nola hadn't seen enough detail to confirm *that,* for which she was glad, but there had certainly been a lot of blood, so she believed it.

Mrs. Russell let out a low moan. "This can't be happening. What do we do?"

"We need to call the police." Anna seemed all business now, and began walking briskly down the hall toward the front desk. The other three women hesitated, then followed her, moving almost as one. Nola figured none of them wanted to be left behind with the body, even if the door was shut.

"Hold on," Mrs. Russell said as Anna rounded the desk and reached for a landline phone. "If someone stabbed him, then that means he was murdered, doesn't it? Which means someone attacked him. Someone who's still here. A guest." Her eyes narrowed in Anna's direction. "Or an employee."

"I'm the only employee who hasn't left yet," Anna said, sounding bitter. "What are you implying?"

"Just that my brother-in-law had been *murdered* and his killer is still here." She looked around, meeting each of their gazes in turn. "Maybe even by one of you. My cabin's right at the end of the row, and I haven't seen anyone leave since the storm began. Unless the person who killed him left on foot, they're still here."

An uncomfortable silence descended on them. Nola shifted, a part of her disbelieving. This couldn't really be happening, could it? But she had seen the dead man. She had seen the blood.

"We need to alert the other guests," Anna decided abruptly. "I will call the other cabins, and ask everyone to come here. Then I'll call the police. You three explain what's going on. If anyone is missing, we will find out soon enough."

It turned out that other than Mrs. Russell and Victoria, there was only one other pair of guests currently staying here besides Nola's own family. Anna greeted them as "Mr. and Mrs. Smith," which sounded like something out of a spy movie to Nola, but it was realistically a very common name. It probably only stood out to her because Mrs. Russell had planted the idea that one of their number was a murderer in her mind.

After requesting the mystery couple's presence at the lobby, Anna made a similar call to Nola's parents' cabin, then to the one she and Henry were staying in. She belatedly realized she should have offered to talk to her family and Henry herself, because they were sure to worry about her otherwise, but the opportunity had passed. It wasn't as if it would take them long to get here, anyway.

Then Anna called the police, dialing a local number instead of 911. She curled the phone cord around her finger and turned slightly away from them as it rang.

Before the dispatcher answered, the door to the lobby opened and Henry came in. Nola rushed over to hug him, feeling something inside her crack. She hadn't realized how tense she had been. With his arms around her and him whispering into her ear, asking what was wrong, she had to blink rapidly to keep her eyes from filling with tears.

Her parents and sister were the next to show up, followed by the mystery couple, who introduced themselves as Hailey and Anthony Smith. Mrs. Russell took over, urging them all to sit down, and promising she would explain what had happened now that they were all here. Before she got a chance to, however, Anna approached, the phone back in its cradle behind the desk.

"I have bad news," she announced to the room at large. "The mountain roads are currently impassable, and the local police are already stretched thin dealing with weather-related emergencies. They do not think they will be able to send anyone up here for at least forty-eight hours, possibly longer."

A beat of silence followed that, until Nola's father said, "I don't understand. What's going on?"

Then Mrs. Russell told them that someone had murdered her brother-in-law, and the room erupted into chaos.

CHAPTER FOUR

"So, you're saying a dead man is shut in the laundry room, and the person who killed him is sitting in here with us?" Nola's father snapped.

"Don't get angry, dear," her mother said. "That's not going to help anything."

"I have a perfectly good reason to be angry. My daughter is one of the people who found the body!"

They were all clustered in the sitting area in the lobby. Ashley gave Nola a sideways glance, and she wrinkled her nose at her sister. She didn't appreciate being dragged into all of this by her father.

"No one is missing," Anna said, looking at each of them. They had all had to go around and introduce themselves, and Anna had compared the names to her list of guests. "Everyone who is supposed to be here is here. I don't like it any more than you do, but just look at it outside. There's a very small window in which Frank could have been killed, and it's not as if we are getting random hikers coming through in the middle of a blizzard. Setting out from here on foot in this weather would be suicide, and someone would have noticed another vehicle arriving and then leaving. The only vehicles which arrived since the last time Frank was seen alive belong to the Shepherds."

All eyes turned to Nola's family. Henry's arm tightened around her shoulder.

"Well, we didn't have anything to do with it," Nola managed to get out. "We've never even been here before! We have no reason to hurt anyone."

"I'm not saying you did," Anna retorted. "I'm just saying, the only possible suspects are the people in this room."

"Now, hold on," Mrs. Russell said. "You're not saying we are *all* suspects, are you? He was my brother-in-law, for goodness sakes. I'm going to have to tell Robert what happened. He's going to be utterly devastated."

"We shouldn't be suspects either," Hailey said, clinging to her husband's hand. "This is our first time here too. We just wanted a nice getaway to celebrate the holiday together."

"I'm sure they're not trying to accuse us of murder," Anthony said, giving Anna a hard glare as he pulled his wife a little closer to his chest.

Anna sighed. "Can everyone please just listen to me? I'm not accusing anyone, individually, of anything. I'm pointing out that the pool of suspects is limited, and unless there is someone on the property that we're unaware of, the killer is in this room. If you would have let me finish, I was going to suggest that we all talk about what to do next. We need to make sure everyone stays safe, and that Frank's body remains undisturbed. The police asked me to lock the room Frank is in, so their investigation can proceed unimpeded after the storm clears."

"I don't see what there is to talk about," Nola's father said. "Obviously, we're all leaving." He looked around the room. "Right?"

Beside Nola, Henry frowned. Before he could say anything, Anna spoke up again.

"Absolutely not! Did you hear what I said? The mountain roads are impassable. If you try to get a vehicle out of here, even one that has four-wheel-drive, you're going to end up stuck or worse. It could be days before someone gets out there to rescue you. No, everyone needs to stay put. We have plenty of firewood, all of the cabins have fireplaces, and we have fresh water and dried goods stored in the pantry. Even if we lose power here, worst case scenario is that we all rough it for a couple of days. Worst case scenario if you go out there and get stuck in a snow drift, is that you freeze to death."

"Worst case scenario if we stay here is that some crazy slasher murders us in our sleep," Victoria said, chiming in for the first time.

She was the only one here who didn't know any of the others, and Nola felt a pang of sympathy for her. It was bad enough having to deal with all of this with her family at her side, but at least she knew none of her family members or Henry was behind the murder. Poor Victoria didn't have anyone she could trust.

"Which is why we need to figure out a safety plan!" The room fell silent at Anna's shout, and the woman took a deep breath to calm herself before continuing.

"I propose that we utilize the buddy system from here on out. No one goes anywhere alone. Of course, couples and families should stay together." She nodded at the Smiths, then at Nola's family. "Which leaves Mrs. Russell, myself and... Victoria, wasn't it?"

Victoria scowled. "Thanks, but no thanks. I don't know either of you. I'm going to feel a lot safer alone in my cabin with the door locked than I would wandering around with two strangers. Aren't most murders committed by someone who knows the victim? That means the two of you are probably the most likely suspects."

Nola exchanged a glance with Henry. That little tidbit *did* sound familiar. She suddenly wished they had watched more true crime shows together.

"How about everyone just does what feels best for themselves?" Anthony asked. Beside him, Hailey nodded. "Those of us who are with someone they trust can do the buddy system, but it doesn't make sense to require it, when you might just end up pairing someone with the murderer."

Nola's father nodded reluctantly. He had been having a whispered argument with her mother, who seemed to have won, judging from the relieved expression on her face. "Since it sounds like it's unsafe to leave, it might be best if we all just stay with the people we know already. If someone's alone, they might be safer being alone than with the wrong person."

Anna sighed. "At least it sounds like you've seen reason. No one is planning on leaving?"

Hailey and Anthony shook their heads. Mrs. Russell just frowned, Victoria didn't respond, and Nola just glanced towards her parents. Sure, she and Henry had their own vehicle here, but if her parents and Ashley decided to try to make it back to town, there was no way she was going to stay behind. She would drive herself crazy with worry about them.

"We're staying," her mother said firmly. "I appreciate what you're trying to do, Anna, but I agree with my husband. I think it's probably best if everyone keeps to their own groups."

Most of the others seemed to share that consensus, and people started making moves to get up. Anna quickly said, "Wait, wait. What about the body? We need to make sure no one messes with it."

"Can't you just lock the room and hold on to the key?" Mrs. Russell snapped. "You're the only employee here, it seems like it should be your job."

Anna flushed, though Nola thought it was more out of anger than embarrassment. "And make myself a target to the killer, if they realize the need to get back into the room for some reason? I don't think so."

Mrs. Russell seemed to be preparing herself to further the argument, but something occurred to Nola, and she spoke up before she could second guess herself.

"Wait, so there's no reason anyone should need to get into the room until the police come, right?" she asked. She felt self-conscious when every eye in the room immediately landed on her.

"The police specifically requested that no one enters the room, for any reason," Anna clarified.

"So, why not just lock the door and slide the key under it?" she suggested. "I'm sure the police can get a locksmith out here once the roads clear, and that way there would be no way any of us can go in and mess with the body, and no one would be a target because they're holding onto the key. We'd all know where it was, but none of us would be able to get to it."

There was a moment of silence. Henry gave her an impressed look. Finally, Mrs. Russell, who seemed to be somewhat in charge, nodded.

"That sounds like a good idea. Let's go do that right now. We can all watch to make sure no one slips the key away secretly, then we'll go our own ways and keep out of each other's hair until the police are able to clear the roads and get up here." She bowed her head. "I need to get back to my cabin and try to contact Robert. He needs to know what happened to his brother."

That seemed to be it; no one else tried to argue, at least. They all gathered in the hallway around the door to the laundry room, watching somberly as Anna locked the door. She tried the knob to show it was locked. Victoria stepped forward to try it as well, and nodded. No one else seemed curious, so Anna knelt down and with a quick flick of her wrist, sent the key sliding under the door with enough force that it must have made it halfway across the room on the other side.

A beat of silence followed, then without another word, the group dispersed.

It was only after stepping outside into the cold that Nola realized she was now consigned to life without towels until they could get out of here.

CHAPTER FIVE

The five of them went to her parents' cabin for a family meeting. Nola hardly noticed the cold walk back this time, probably because she already felt numb with shock. They stamped their boots as they went through the door and took a few moments to peel off their outerwear in silence. Finally, they gathered in the small living area to talk. Ashley ended up perching on the arm of the couch, next to Nola, while her father stood behind where her mother sat in the armchair. Nola and Henry had the couch – a loveseat, really – and were clinging onto each other's hands. In fact, Nola thought she hadn't let go of his hand since leaving the lobby, other than when they took their gloves off.

"I still think we should leave," her father said after taking a deep breath. He squeezed her mother's shoulder before she could argue. "I think we should put it to a vote. We're all adults here, and we should all get a say. Whatever we end up doing, though, I want us to do it together. We either all go, or all stay. Agreed?"

Nola nodded. She had been thinking the same thing herself earlier.

"I agree with that part," her mother said. "But I don't think it's a good idea to try to leave. If the police can't get up the mountain, we aren't going to have a chance at getting down it. And that woman was right – if something goes wrong, no one is coming to rescue us, not in this weather."

"I don't know what I want to do," Ashley admitted. "I mean, if someone who's staying here really did kill that man, it's probably dangerous to stick around, but at the same time, we know for a fact that the weather is dangerous. I guess it makes more sense to stay? If we leave, we'd be going from a potential danger to a certain danger."

"I think we should stay as well," Henry said, giving Nola's hand a squeeze. "But I'll do whatever Nola prefers. I don't like the thought of going out there, but I don't think any of us are going to rest easy while we're here either."

"Sorry, Dad," Nola said, glancing at her father. "I'm voting we stay as well. We barely made it up here, and the weather's just gotten worse."

"All right," her father said, bowing his head. "That settles it, then. I'll respect what everyone else decided. We'll stay."

"How long is this storm supposed to last, exactly?" Ashley asked. "Did anyone even check the weather before we left?"

"Henry and I did," Nola said. "It's supposed to storm through tomorrow, and die off sometime tomorrow night. But it wasn't supposed to start storming until later, so maybe it's moving faster than it was supposed to? That might mean it will be over sooner."

"It also might mean the storm has gotten worse," her father added. "I know we all packed some food. We should probably try to make it last."

"Speaking of food," Nola's mother said. "I was just about to get dinner started when we got that call to go to the lobby. And weren't the two of you going to make something for dessert? I know it's been a crazy evening, but we still have to eat."

There was a strange return to normalcy after that. Nola's mother went into the kitchen, and Nola and Henry ducked back over to their cabin to grab the pie Henry had popped into the oven before the fiasco at the lobby happened.

Whenever someone brought up the murder, her mother hushed them. As a result, they had a quiet dinner together that felt normal, if a bit forced. Only after washing the dishes did they return to talking about what had happened.

"So, Nola, did you notice anything weird when you saw the dead guy?" Ashley asked.

"*Ashley*," her mother hissed.

"What? I'm just asking. Shouldn't we be trying to figure out who killed him?"

"I only got a glimpse," Nola said. "But Anna, the woman who works here, she said it looked like he had been stabbed."

"I hate thinking of you going through that alone," Henry said. "I wish I had come with you. But I guess there's no way any of us could have known what was going to happen."

"Ashley does have a point," Nola's father said. "One of the other guests here is potentially a very dangerous person. Since we don't know who to avoid, we should keep to ourselves. The buddy system that other woman brought up was a good idea. Nola and Henry, I'm assuming you two will keep an eye on each other. And your mother and I will keep each other in sight, of course. Ashley, will you agree to always either be with me and your mother, or your sister and Henry?"

"I'm twenty-four, Dad. You sound like I'm an eight-year-old going to a theme park for the first time. But yeah, I'm not an idiot. None of us should go anywhere alone. Like, probably not even right next door. That's pretty much the first rule of horror movies, isn't it? Never go anywhere alone."

"And if one of the other guest tries to come in to either of our cabins, we should politely turn them down," her mother said. "We can't afford to let the wrong person in."

As they laid down the ground rules to make sure their family stayed safe, Nola felt herself begin to relax incrementally. Frank's body was a horrible thing to have stumbled across, but as long as she and her family sat tight and didn't take any risks for the next few days, they should be able to get through this holiday without anyone getting hurt.

Then the power went out. There was no warning, no flickering of lights or sudden buzz of a surge. One moment, the furnace and fridge were humming merrily and the overhead light was bathing them in a warm glow, and the next they were plunged into silent darkness.

Nola swore she felt the temperature in the room drop by a couple of degrees just in the few, stunned seconds that followed.

"Liam?" Her mother's voice was tight and sharp in the darkness. "You did say this place has generators, right?"

"The website advertised a backup generator in case of power outages," her father said.

They all sat silently for another moment, but the power did not return. Nola shot a glance toward the fireplace, where the fire her father had made earlier was giving off a dull glow. It was just embers now, and barely gave off any light.

A chilling thought struck her.

"It shouldn't take them this long to come on, should it? What if…" She hesitated, not wanting to worry the others for no reason. But she had already started talking, and felt committed. "What if whoever killed Frank sabotaged the generators too?"

CHAPTER SIX

Using their phone flashlights to guide them, they searched for candles and matches, but didn't find any of the former. There were plenty of the latter, so her father began trying to build up the fire in the fireplace.

While he was busy with that, Nola walked over to the window and looked out, wondering if the generator only powered the main building.

But all she could see outside was snow. It was a white out, or as close to one as she had ever experienced. There was nothing merry about this snowstorm. It felt apocalyptic, as if the entire world was freezing over. Shivering, she tugged the curtains shut.

"Well, this is just great," Ashley said. She hadn't moved from the couch. Nola wondered if she regretted agreeing to come on this trip. She could have been somewhere warm and sunny with her college friends right now. "It's going to storm for at least the next day, and we don't have any power. At least we won't freeze to death, assuming we can actually keep the fire going."

"The pipes are going to burst in those empty cabins without any power," her father muttered. He glanced over at Nola and Henry. "If the two of you want to stay here with us, you are more than welcome to, but we should go over to your cabin and make sure the water is turned off. You don't want to wake up to a flooded cabin in the morning."

She exchanged a look with Henry, who squeezed her hand, letting her know it was her choice. It might be safer to stay here with her parents and Ashley, but it would be cramped – there was only the one bedroom, and the couch didn't pull out — even if it did, Ashley had already claimed it — so she and Henry would have to sleep on the living room floor.

She didn't think she and Henry would be that much less safe on their own. It wouldn't be hard to lock the cabin up tight, and they wouldn't go anywhere alone. It would be a lot more comfortable, and it would have the added benefit of keeping their cabin warm. That way they wouldn't have to worry about burst pipes, or about carrying all of their things over here.

"I think we'll head back to our place," she said. "But I have my phone on me, so –" She broke off, realizing they couldn't call her. Without power, they didn't have Wi-Fi, and without Wi-Fi, they didn't have any way to contact each other.

Her father looked worried for a second, but then something seemed to occur to him. He stood up, fanning the little fire in the fireplace one last time before hurrying into the other room. He returned a moment later with two walkie-talkies. After turning them both on, he handed one to her and pushed the talk button on his. "Testing, can you hear me?"

She winced at the squeal of interference that came through with his words, but dutifully tested hers out too. It worked.

"I didn't know you brought these. We've had them forever."

"I figured we might want to split off into different groups while we're here, and I didn't know how good the cell service up in the mountains would be. You and Henry take that, and we'll keep the other one. Keep it on; I brought a pack of batteries too, so don't worry about it dying. This way, we can keep in touch even if the power doesn't come back on."

She handed the walkie-talkie to Henry, who seemed thrilled to examine it. "Thanks, Dad," she said. She gave her parents and her sister tight hugs, then she and Henry got their winter gear back on and stepped out into the cold.

She couldn't even see their cabin, even though it was right next door. There was an eerie moment when they were halfway between both cabins when all she could see was white. Then she took a few more steps and the shadowy form of their cabin resolved itself.

They let themselves inside, stomping their boots to get the excess snow off. She felt a prickle of unease when she realized the door was unlocked. There had been no reason for Henry to lock it when he thought all he had to do was pop over to the main building for an announcement, so she didn't blame him, but she still felt unsettled.

"Let's check through the closets and under the beds before we relax," she whispered to him. He nodded grimly, making a detour to the kitchen to pick up a frying pan. She grabbed a broom from the pantry as her makeshift weapon, holding her phone to act as a flashlight in her other hand.

They searched the little cabin together, checking every nook and cranny. Thankfully, it was empty, and their items were undisturbed. She double-checked the door and the windows, making sure everything was locked tight before she pulled the curtains shut. Henry was already getting a fire going in the fireplace, but even if they got it roaring, it was going to be a cold night. She slipped into the bedroom to begin dragging the mattress into the living room. It was a far cry from sleeping on the floor, but they were still going to be roughing it. She was never going to take central heating for granted again.

A little while later, the walkie talkie crackled with a goodnight message from her parents, and she curled up with Henry on the mattress in front of the fireplace. It was almost cozy, despite the knowledge that a murderer might be lingering just outside their cabin door. She felt safe, snuggled into Henry's arms, and soon, she drifted off to sleep.

She woke up sometime during the night to see the fire burning low. Henry was snoring beside her, and she knew nothing short of an earthquake was going to wake him up right now. She slipped out of the blankets, wincing at the cold air outside of her little cocoon. Quietly, she crept over to the fireplace and put two new logs on top of the embers. They caught fire quickly, giving more light to the room.

The sound of an engine outside made her look up, though the curtains were still closed. Maybe that was what had woken her, and not the low fire. Had the police sent someone up after all?

She hurried over to the window, pulling the curtain aside. It was still snowing hard, but it had eased up enough that she could see a few feet into the parking lot. The glowing red taillights of an SUV were impossible to miss.

The engine whined again, and she realized that the person had bottomed out their vehicle in the snow. It wasn't moving an inch, no matter how much the wheels spun. She frowned, wondering who had decided to try to leave at a time like this.

The person tried again, sending a flurry of snow up behind the vehicle, but it wasn't helping. They were well and truly stuck.

She wondered if the person needed help. They could just give up and walk back to their cabin, but maybe they were so determined to leave because they had been hurt and needed to get to a hospital, or they had a family emergency. She would feel bad ignoring them now that she had noticed their vehicle.

Putting the curtain shut again, she hurried back over to Henry and started shaking his shoulder. "Henry," she hissed. "Henry, wake up. Someone's outside, and I think they're stuck."

He blinked his eyes open blearily, and she had to explain what was going on a few times before his sleepy mind realized where they were and what was happening. When he finally joined her at the window, the person was still struggling with their vehicle. He frowned at them for a second.

"Guess we should go see if they need something," he said at last.

"It's the right thing to do," she agreed. "But is it the smart thing to do?" She had woken him up for this, but now that the prospect of actually going out into the snowy night to help a possibly murderous stranger was right in front of her, she was having some doubts.

"If they were looking for another victim, I don't think they'd be sitting in their car in the middle of a parking lot," he pointed out. "Even if they *are* the killer, they'd probably just be grateful if we can get them unstuck. Better yet, if they are the killer and they're able to leave, it would make *everyone* safer."

She hesitated a moment longer, but he had a point, and she wasn't sure either of them would be able to get back to sleep with the sound of the stuck vehicle's engine whining every time the driver tried to get it free. They got dressed in their winter gear in the scant light from the fire, then stepped outside. The wind and snow might have died down a little, but it was frigid, cold enough so that when Nola breathed in, it felt like her lungs were freezing solid.

They carefully navigated the buried steps and waded through the snow toward the SUV. The driver must not have seen them because they spun their wheels again, sending a spray of snow right into Nola's face. Henry knocked on the back window and they stopped, leaving her sputtering.

They made their way around to the driver's side window, which rolled down an inch so the woman inside could talk to them. Victoria. It looked like she had been crying, but whether out of fear or frustration or something else, Nola didn't know. She thought being stuck in the snow in a resort in the middle of nowhere with an unknown killer roaming around must be a special kind of nightmare.

"What?" Victoria snapped.

"You're not going anywhere," Henry said. "Your car is bottomed out. If you've got a shovel, maybe we can help dig you free, but I don't think it's a good idea."

"You don't understand," Victoria said, her voice laced with panic. "I need to get out of here."

"You're just going to run out of gas," Henry said. "Or you're going to overheat your engine. You should head back to your cabin. Maybe we can dig the parking lot out when the snow stops."

"They probably have a shovel in the main building," Victoria said, biting her lip. "They must have one *somewhere*. Will you help me dig my car out if I can find one? I can't stay until the storm ends. I just can't."

"I don't think that's a good idea," Nola said. "The roads aren't going to be any better than this. You'll just get stuck again."

"Then I'll bring the shovel with me," Victoria said. "If you don't want to help, that's fine, but I'm going to get out of here tonight one way or the other."

Nola and Henry exchanged a glance, a silent agreement passing between them. They had each other, at least. Victoria had no one. Nola couldn't even imagine how terrified she must be, without a single person she could trust in this situation. They turned back to her, nodding.

"We'll help you get your car unstuck, at least," Nola said.

Victoria rolled up the window and shut the engine off before getting out of the car. She went around to the back and opened the hatch.

"What are you doing?" Nola asked, shuffling her feet in an attempt to keep warm. They felt like icicles, even inside of her boots.

"My luggage," Victoria said. "I don't want to leave it out here."

"No one's going to steal it," Nola said. "Just lock your car and let's go find a shovel. It's freezing out here."

The other woman hesitated, then slammed the hatch and locked the vehicle with her key fob. She was less warmly dressed than Nola and Henry, and blew into her ungloved hands, her teeth chattering.

"A-alright," she said, shivering. "To the lobby?"

Nola nodded and the three of them turned toward the lobby lights. Only a few steps later, Nola faltered. She looked over at Henry, and his eyes widened slightly as he realized the same thing she had.

The lobby lights. That meant the generator was working, and the lobby had power.

CHAPTER SEVEN

She wasn't sure if the lobby lights had been on before, and she just hadn't been able to see them through the snow, or if they had come on at some point after she and Henry fell asleep. Either way, there was no denying that they were on now. As they neared the building, the blob of light defined itself into warm, glowing windows. Even closer, and she could hear the chug of the generator.

The cabins might not have power, but it was a relief all the same. Stepping into the lobby was like stepping out of a dream and back into real life. The air was warm, the overhead lights buzzed gently, and the quiet sound of someone talking on the phone in the other room welcomed them in.

She had spent only a few hours without power – most of them asleep – but apparently that was more than enough, because she felt an almost physical sensation of relief once she was inside the building.

The three of them clustered just inside the door. The space behind the front desk was empty, as usual, but the door behind it was cracked open. In fact, the entire main room of the lobby was empty. She glanced down the hall, but the door to the laundry room was still shut. Trying not to think about what exactly was behind that door, she looked around, trying to figure out where a shovel might be kept.

"They must keep the outdoor supplies in a storage room somewhere," Victoria murmured, keeping her voice low.

"We should probably let Anna know we're here," Nola said. "I don't want to surprise her, especially not after what happened to her boss."

Henry nodded his agreement and they headed toward the front desk, since the sound of a phone conversation was coming from the room behind it. She paused as she rounded the desk, noticing that the land line's cord was stretched into the other room – whoever was on the phone was using the landline, not their cell phone. It was good news the phone lines weren't down, not that it did them much good, since it had been made clear there would be no help from emergency services for another day, at least.

She frowned as she heard what the person on the other side of the door was saying.

"I know, sweetie, and I'm sorry. I hate that I had to travel so close to Christmas, but you know how demanding this job is. There's absolutely no way I'm going to get home on time. This storm is crazy. The land lines are down and my phone is dead, so I'm borrowing an employee's cell phone to call you, but she's going to go home soon, so if you need to get in touch with me, just leave a message on my cell and I'll get back to you whenever I can charge it. I'll try to call you again tomorrow." She paused. "Love you too. Bye-bye."

Nola exchanged a glance with Henry. Something about what they had overheard seemed off. She raised her hand and knocked on the partially open door. The woman on the other side made a soft sound of surprise and reached over to pull the door open.

"You surprised me," the woman said. It wasn't Anna, as Nola had expected. It was Hailey, the woman who was here with her husband.

But that didn't make any sense. She was on a romantic getaway, not for work. And she had just said the landlines were down, but the receiver was still in her hand. Nola frowned, and the other woman's expression turned stiff.

"Do you need to use the phone?" she asked. "I needed to make a personal call, but I'm done now. You're welcome to use it."

"No thanks, we were looking for Anna," Nola said.

Shrugging, Hailey stood up and edged past Nola, Henry, and Victoria so she could return the landline phone to its cradle behind the front desk. The sound of a toilet flushing drew Nola's attention back to the lobby just in time to see Anthony come out of one of the restrooms.

The two of them talked quietly as they gathered up their winter gear. They must have noticed that the lobby had power, and stopped in to use the restroom and make a call. Nola frowned as she watched them get ready to leave. The call she overheard hadn't made sense. She shook her head, trying to refocus on the issue at hand.

"Hold on," she called before they could step out the door. "There's a vehicle stuck in the parking lot. Have either of you seen Anna? We're looking for a shovel to dig it out, but we don't want to poke around too much without talking to her first."

"She was in the kitchen last I saw," Anthony called out to her. He held the door open for Hailey, who seemed in a rush to leave. "Good luck. I wouldn't go anywhere tonight if I were you."

With that, the two of them left. Victoria turned down the hall.

"I guess the kitchen is probably that way?"

"It must be," Nola said. "At least we know for sure what room it *isn't* in."

The kitchen, it turned out, was right next to the laundry room, and had a delicious scent of blueberries cooking coming from it. She knocked lightly and pushed the door open, revealing Anna, who was taking a tray of muffins out of the oven. The woman jumped a little when she saw Nola and the others looking in at her.

"Oh, you startled me," She hesitated, glancing between Nola, Henry, and Victoria. "I'd be most comfortable if you stayed out of the kitchen," she said, putting a hand on her hip. "No offense, but I'm still spooked by what happened."

"Right," Nola said, pausing in the doorway. "Sorry. You couldn't sleep?"

Anna sighed, looking down at the tray of muffins she had just taken out. "No, I couldn't. I thought I'd do some baking so there's some fresh food in the morning. The generator's only got enough fuel for about twelve hours. I'm going to use it sparingly, but there's no guarantee of when the power will come back on, so I thought preparing food that will keep would be the best thing to do. What can I help you with?"

"We're looking for a shovel," Victoria said from behind Nola. "I'm trying to dig my SUV out of the snow."

Anna made a face. "You're not really trying to go somewhere in this weather, are you?"

"Can you please just tell me where the shovels are?" Victoria asked, her tone indicating she was quickly running out of patience. "I don't need another person telling me what to do."

Anna's shoulders slumped. "We keep them in a shed out back. Normally, I'd tell you to follow the path to the edge of the woods, but you're never going to find it in this snow. You're better off waiting until morning. It's locked, anyway – Frank's the one who kept the keys for all of that. I'd have to look through his office to see if I can find them, but it's possible he had them on him."

There was a tense silence from Victoria. Nola gave Anna a weak smile. "Thanks. We'll just have to try once the weather clears up. We'll leave you be now."

Shutting the kitchen door, she turned to face the others in the hall. Victoria had her arms crossed and her lips pressed together. Henry just looked tired – she had a feeling he still hadn't fully woken up.

"Sorry, Victoria, but it really sounds like this isn't going to happen tonight. Do you feel unsafe in your cabin?" She wasn't sure if she wanted to offer their own cabin up to the woman, but she felt horrible for her. She knew she would be absolutely terrified if she was in this situation alone.

"I'll just have to deal with it," Victoria said. "Thanks for offering to help, though. I appreciate it."

They left the lobby, venturing back into the snow. Their path from the vehicle was already almost covered by fresh snowfall. When they reached Victoria's vehicle, she paused by the back hatch, brushing the snow off of the handle before popping it open. Nola and Henry hesitated.

"Do you want help getting your luggage back to your cabin?" Nola asked.

"Thanks, but I've got it handled," Victoria said with a weak smile.

"It's no problem," Harry said.

"No, really," Victoria said. She hesitated. "I just – with everything that's going on, I'm not sure how comfortable I am with anyone following me back to my cabin."

Nola winced, exchanging a guilty look with Henry. She hadn't even thought that they might be making her uncomfortable.

"I'm so sorry," she said. "Of course – whatever you're comfortable with. Just be careful, all right? If you need anything, just shout. I'm sure we'll be up for a while yet."

Victoria gave a stiff nod, and then waited for Nola and Henry to begin walking back to their cabin before she started taking her luggage out.

Nola was glad nothing bad had happened during their misguided attempt to help her, but the result was still chilling. Victoria's vehicle getting stuck had confirmed that there was no way they could get out of the resort until the storm was over. It was a good thing her family had voted to stay, because they wouldn't have been able to leave even if they wanted to.

CHAPTER EIGHT

A crackling whine made Nola's eyelids flutter open. She stared at the glowing embers of the fire, confused and displaced. The crackling sound came again.

"Nola, are you and Henry alive over there?"

Her sister's voice. All of a sudden, the events of the preceding day returned to her. She sat up, turning to tuck the blankets around Henry when he gave a nearly inaudible grumble about the cold, and reached for the walkie-talkie, which she had sat down on the floor next to the mattress. There was enough light coming through the curtains to let her know it was morning, but the day hadn't brought any extra warmth with it. It was freezing in the cabin – not literally, she didn't think, but certainly close to it. She scooted off the mattress and over to the fireplace, plopping a log down on the embers and poking at the coals with a fire poker. Raising the walkie-talkie to her face, she hit the send button.

"Yeah, we just woke up," she said. "What time is it?"

"It's a little after eight," Ashley sighed. "My phone's dead, but Mom's and Dad's still have some charge. Have you looked outside?"

The fire needed some more kindling anyway, so she set the fire poker down and stood up. On her way to the kitchen, where she was planning on deconstructing the paper towel roll, she paused to pull a curtain to the side.

What she found outside stole her breath away. It was still snowing, but visibility was good enough that she could just see the lobby building across the parking lot. The world had transformed overnight. Snow covered absolutely everything. The vehicles in the parking lot were shapeless mounds covered in white, and the drifts against the sides of the vehicles and the buildings were higher than her head in some places. There were no footprints, and the entire parking lot was a pristine snowfield.

It was beautiful. She felt a pang, wishing she could have woken up to this on any other day. Frank's murder cast a pallor over everything.

"Happy Christmas Eve," her sister said through the walkie-talkie. She realized with a start that it really *was* Christmas Eve. She had almost completely forgotten about the holiday.

"Yeah, you too. Are Mom and Dad already up?"

"Yep. They wanted me to see if you two were awake yet, and to see if you wanted to come over for breakfast. Mom brought eggs and bacon, but she's not sure what you guys brought and she wants to try to meal plan."

"The only breakfast thing we have is a box of cereal and a package of some frozen breakfast sausages," Nola said. "Come to think of it, most of what we brought is frozen food. I guess I should probably put it outside – there's no chance it will thaw and go bad out there. I think Henry fell back asleep, and I want to get dressed and do something about my hair. We'll be there in half an hour with the cereal and some milk."

Her sister confirmed that was fine and she put the walkie-talkie down so she could gather some paper towels to use as kindling to prod the fire back to life. Once the log had caught, she stole the blankets from Henry.

"Rise and shine," she said cheerily, throwing the blankets on the couch. "Breakfast waits for no man. Let's get dressed and head over to my parents' cabin. Just wait until you see it outside. It's like the beginning of a new ice age out there."

Twenty minutes later, they made the short, snowy journey over to her parents' cabin. It felt like a shame to mar the beautiful snow, but she was getting hungry. She could smell the bacon even before she walked through the door, and then had to pause to admire her mother's creativity. She had the frying pan propped up on two logs over a bed of embers, with bacon and eggs sizzling away inside of it.

Maybe this whole power outage thing wasn't too bad. They could stay warm, they had food, and if worst came to worst they could melt and boil snow for water. They would survive, it just might not be very fun.

As they ate breakfast together, she and Henry told her parents and her sister about their brief adventure with

Victoria the night before. When her father got up to look out the window to where Victoria's car was still stuck, he turned back to them in surprise.

"There's some people out there shoveling snow," he said. "We should go help them."

"What happened to staying away from everyone so we don't get slashed by the killer?" Ashley asked.

"It's probably better to go with the flow in this case," her father said. "I don't think the killer would be thrilled about us sitting in here on our lazy butts while they shovel our doorstep."

Ashley made a face at that but didn't argue.

The five of them got their winter gear on and went outside. Anna seemed to be leading the shoveling expedition, and directed them to the shed around back to get their own shovels. Someone — probably her — had shoveled a path to it. *She must have found the key in Frank's office,* Nola thought when the door opened easily for them.

Inside were skis, snowshoes, and an entire shelf with ice skates, along with more than enough snow shovels for everyone. They each chose one, then returned to the parking lot to join the others in moving the truly monstrous amounts of snow.

Everyone was out there helping. She spotted Hailey and Anthony shoveling a path between the parking lot and the lobby. Mrs. Russell was carefully clearing off the steps up to her cabin, and Victoria was trying to dig her car out. Anna and Nola's family focused on clearing as much of the parking lot as they could. They might not be able to leave, but being able to walk between the cabins and the lobby freely and maneuver around the parking lot would make things a lot easier.

It took them over two hours to clear the entire parking lot and get the cars cleaned off. Victoria took advantage of the snow removal to move her SUV back to its place in front of her cabin, and seemed relieved when the vehicle started without issue.

Finally done, they gathered into a loose group around Anna, who was leaning on her shovel, her hood pulled back and her brow sweaty. The work had done a lot to warm them up; Nola had even unzipped her coat.

"Whew, that was hard work, but we got a lot done. If anyone wants to go inside and get some coffee, now's your chance. I'm going to shut the generator off in about ten minutes. We've only got another six hours of fuel left, which I intend to conserve. There's plenty of muffins inside, so please help yourselves."

"Are there any books or games we can bring back to our cabin?" Hailey asked. "We were planning on spending a lot of time outside, so we didn't bring much to do."

"We have some games behind the desk, and a box of old magazines you're welcome to help yourselves to," Anna said. "We also have some recreational equipment in the shed behind the main building. If you want to ice skate, you'll have to take shovels with you to clear the lake, and if you're going to snowshoe or ski, please grab one of the area maps and tell someone where you're going first."

"That seems like a bad idea," Mrs. Russell said, scoffing. "Has everyone forgotten that someone here brutally murdered my brother-in-law last night? I don't know about you, but I'm not going to be telling *anyone* where I am, especially not if I'm going into the woods alone. That's just *asking* for trouble."

"Yeah, as much as we were looking forward to hiking, I don't think Anthony and I are quite up to doing it in these circumstances," Hailey said. "Ice-skating might be fun, though. If we all go together, we can keep an eye on each other. Nothing's going to happen if we're in a big group, right?"

"If you want to get a group together to go ice-skating, I'll tag along," Anna said. Hailey turned toward Nola and her family, her expression hopeful.

Nola's family conferred briefly. Her mother wanted to stay in the cabin as a family unit, but everyone else wanted to go, and when Ashley pointed out it was *Christmas Eve,* the argument was won.

Finally, Nola turned back to Hailey. "Sure, I guess we'll go too."

"I suppose it will make the time pass more quickly," Mrs. Russell said with a sigh. "I'm a little rusty, but I'll come along."

"Well, I'm staying here," Victoria said, crossing her arms. "I think you're all crazy, going out there and pretending nothing happened. I'm going to lock myself in my cabin and not budge until we can leave."

"Right, that's it, then," Anna said, clapping her hands. "Everyone except for Victoria is coming down to the lake. We should all remember to stick together."

With that, everyone headed toward the shed to find a pair of ice skates that would fit them. Everyone except for Victoria. Nola paused to watch as she walked back to her cabin, her shovel over her shoulder, and body hunched against the cold air.

A part of her wanted to urge the other woman to come with them, but she had to respect Victoria's wishes. She thought their plan of staying in a big group was probably pretty safe, but Victoria didn't have a single person there she knew and trusted. She could understand why she might be more comfortable on her own.

Unless Victoria had another reason not to be afraid. If she *was* the killer, she wouldn't have anything to worry about.

Nola shook her head, quickly rejoining the others. Victoria didn't have any more of a motive to murder Frank than Nola did. No, if one of the people here *had* killed him, it was most likely to be one of the two woman who knew him – either Anna or Mrs. Russell, his employee and his sister-in-law, respectively.

Maybe one of them would let something slip during the ice-skating expedition, and then they could put the question of who they could trust to rest. With that thought giving a new spring to her thoughts, she hurried ahead to pick out her ice skates.

CHAPTER NINE

The walk down to the lake almost felt festive. It was still snowing, fat merry flakes that seemed like something out of a storybook, and the boughs of the pine trees hung low under their load. Everywhere except where they walked was pristine, untouched white.

In another circumstance, it might have been Nola's best Christmas Eve yet.

She was glad Anna had come with them, because the lake was a flat expanse of snow, and she wasn't sure she would have been able to tell where it began without the other woman guiding them. Working together, they cleared a sizeable patch of the frozen lake, leaving smooth ice that was practically begging for skates.

They kept mostly to their own groups at first, but as time went on and the infrequent ice skaters regained their confidence, some of the invisible boundaries seemed to shatter, and people began to skate around the makeshift rink without caring who they were next to.

With everyone together in a group like this, it was hard to imagine something bad happening. Frank had been killed in secret; his killer would have to be insane to try something in plain sight of the rest of the guests.

Panting and with legs like jelly, Nola took a break from ice skating and made her way over to a fallen log not far from the cleared patch of ice. Mrs. Russell, who had skated for only a few minutes before retiring, had brushed the snow off the top of it, and it made for a comfortable seat.

Nola sat down a few feet away from the other woman, her eyes still on the lake. When Henry started skating toward her, a question in his eyes like he was wondering if she wanted him to join her, she waved him away. He looked like he was still having fun; she would rejoin him soon, she just wanted a breather.

"Look at them all," Mrs. Russell said from beside her, tsking. "As if a man isn't lying dead not a quarter of a mile away from us. Of course, *they* don't have to worry about telling my precious Robert his brother has passed on. *They* don't have to think beyond sitting out this storm and scurrying back home where they can forget this ever happened."

Nola glanced over at her, feeling awkward. "I'm sorry. I can't imagine how hard this is for you. I think we're all just trying not to think about what happened. There's nothing we can do, after all, and this is a good outlet for everyone's stress."

The older woman scoffed. "There's nothing we can do? I beg to differ. We could be trying to figure out who murdered my brother-in-law, instead of skating in circles. I thought this would be better than sitting alone in my cabin, but if anything, it's worse. What am I supposed to tell Robert when he gets back and learns what happened?"

"Robert's your husband?" Nola asked. Mrs. Russell nodded. "Do the two of you live here?"

She shook her head. "No, we were just visiting Frank for Christmas. He's up here at the resort year-round, and hates leaving it, so we always came to stay in a cabin up here a couple times a year and help out where we could." She pursed her lips. "Frank was always taking advantage of Robert's good heart. The night the storm hit, he sent Robert into town to pick up more fuel for the generator, even though it had already begun to snow! Thank goodness he was able to call me from town before we lost power, or else I would be a wreck right now, but he ended up having to stay at a motel to wait out the storm. I hate to think about what would have happened if he tried to drive back up here when the blizzard was at its worst."

The sound of crunching snow made Nola look up. Anna was coming over, walking awkwardly across the ground in her skates.

"It's a shame he didn't make it back before the storm hit," she said as she joined them on the log. "We could have used that fuel. Frank, may he rest in peace, never took storms like this seriously."

Her expression twisted into something bitter, and Mrs. Russell gave her a surprisingly empathetic look.

"You were supposed to be spending the holiday with your family, weren't you, Anna? I remember Frank telling us he wouldn't have any help over the holiday."

Anna sniffed. "I was *supposed* to be at my sister's house. She just had her first baby, and I was going to spend the week with her. Frank insisted I stay late and help prepare for the storm, and now I'm stranded here. The man drove me mad sometimes."

Mrs. Russell gave a tremulous smile. "He drove me mad too. He didn't have a reasonable bone in his body, I swear..."

As the two of them reminisced over Frank in their oddly insulting way, Nola murmured an excuse and rose to her feet, making her way back toward the lake. She felt like she was intruding.

Henry skated over to her to help her onto the ice, and they skated in a slow circle around the makeshift rink together. Nola was considering going over to Ashley and asking if she wanted to race when she saw Anthony wipe out, overbalancing a turn and careening into the pile of snow at the edge of the cleared area.

Everyone skated over to him, and he grimaced as Hailey helped him up.

"Thanks, honey," he said. "That was embarrassing. Nothing to see here, people. Let's just pretend that didn't happen."

He and his wife skated away. Nola turned to resume her own lazy circles around the lake, but something in the snow where Henry had fallen caught her eyes.

A black leather square that turned out to be a wallet when she got closer. Holding Henry's hand for balance, she bent over to pick it up.

"Must have fallen out of his pocket when he took a tumble," he said.

"Yeah, let's go give it back to him. It's lucky we saw it; I doubt he would have ever found it otherwise."

As she lifted the wallet, it flipped open and her eyes landed on his ID. *Anthony Anderson.* She frowned. Hadn't he and Hailey introduced themselves as the Smiths?

She remembered the phone call of Hailey's she had overheard. Something about them was definitely off, but she wasn't sure how to learn more without drawing attention to herself.

A couple with something to hide might be a couple who was willing to kill to keep their secret.

CHAPTER TEN

They skated for hours before finally making their way back up to the resort. Nola was exhausted down to her bones, and everyone else seemed to feel similarly.

Despite the circumstances of Frank's murder, strange camaraderie had grown between them during their ice-skating expedition, and before they reached the parking lot and dispersed to their own cabins, Anna halted to address them.

"I'm sure we're all hungry," she said. "If you're interested, I can turn the generator back on for an hour, and we can make a potluck meal together. If everyone contributes a little, we'll have plenty to go around, and I'm sure we would all like a chance to warm up in the main building instead trying to get fires going in your cabins."

After huddling for another quick family discussion, Nola's father agreed, and they all went toward the lobby together. The building was chilly, but soon after Anna vanished down the hall, the generator kicked to life and the power came back on. The furnace started kicking out heat, and Hailey and Anthony made a beeline for one of the vents, huddling in front of it. Mrs. Russell sat down on the armchair in the common area, while Ashley and Nola's father started making a fire in the big fireplace while Nola's mother watched, a little bemused.

"Hold on, now," Anna said as she came back into the room. "Don't get too comfortable. We all have to contribute. Everyone needs to bring some food to share. And someone should go get that other woman, too. She should at least know what we're doing, even if she doesn't want to join us."

"Ashley, if you want to come with me, we can pop over to the cabin with Nola and Henry and get some food," Nola's mother said. "I think your father is too engrossed with the fire to want to come with me."

Her father waved a hand and muttered something incomprehensible as he built up a perfect little teepee of kindling.

The four of them walked out of the main building together, but Nola paused before they reached the cabins. "We should probably go let Victoria know what's happening," she said. "Anna's right; she deserves to know, even if she doesn't want to join us. You two go on ahead, Henry and I will catch up."

"We could just let someone else take care of it," Henry pointed out as they changed course to the cabin at the end of the row. "I don't get the feeling she's going to be eager to join the potluck."

"I figured she might be more comfortable with us than the others, since we helped her out last night," Nola explained.

He nodded, and they walked through the parking lot together. There were another couple inches of snow on the ground, but it was nowhere near as bad as it had been when they woke up that morning. She was glad they had taken the time to clear the snow – it had been hard work, but it was worth it now. They made their way down to the end of the row of cabins together, and Nola climbed the steps with Henry right behind her. She knocked on the cabin door and waited for Victoria to open it.

It took the other woman long enough that Nola began to worry that she wasn't going to answer at all. Finally, the door pulled open, revealing a messy cabin behind Victoria. Nola squinted at the mess, wondering what on earth had happened. Victoria's fluffy winter coat was missing a sleeve, and there was an open sewing kit on the table and other clothes strewn about.

"Are you all right?" she blurted out.

Victoria gave her a sour look, shifting to block most of her view of the room. "I'm fine. What do you want?"

"Everyone's making dinner together at the main building," she said, forcing herself not to try to peep past Victoria's shoulder. "We wanted to let you know, just in case you want to join us."

"What part of *I want to be left alone* do you people not understand?" Victoria asked. "It was nice of you to think of me, but please, just leave me out of this. I'm going to keep to myself until I can leave."

"All right," Nola said, backing up a step. "Sorry. If you change your mind, you're welcome to join us."

"I'll think about it," Victoria said in a tone of voice that told Nola she probably wouldn't. She shut the door and Nola heard the sound of the lock turning.

With a sigh, she turned and walked down the steps, careful not to slip on the snow-slick wood. Henry took her hand and gave it a reassuring squeeze.

"Everyone's on edge," he reminded her. "She's been cooped up in there alone all day, so it's probably worse for her. I think ice skating took the edge off for the rest of us."

"You're right," she said. "Let's go grab some food to share with everyone. I'm starving."

Dinner was a mishmash of random dishes. Anna made some mashed potatoes from a box of dried potato flakes, Mrs. Russell had brought bratwurst and buns, Nola and Henry supplied a box of frozen jalapeno poppers, and her parents sacrificed an entire rotisserie chicken. Nola hadn't even realized they had brought a whole chicken with them.

The kitchen was large enough that they could all gather in it, though only had enough counter space for one or two people to work over the stove at once. Nola offered to wash the dishes as people cooked, and tried not to think about Frank's murder as she scrubbed the black-handled kitchen knives. Was one of them the murder weapon? No, it was better not to dwell on it.

No one seemed eager to go off alone, and Nola couldn't blame them. There was something comfortable about being in a group like this, despite the paranoia that came from knowing that any one of their number might be the killer. Together, there was a certain sense of safety that vanished when they returned to solitude.

They gathered in the lobby to eat, loading paper plates with food and settling into seats in front of the roaring fire Nola's father had built up. Anna turned off the generator to conserve the rest of the fuel, but brought out candles, so the room was lit with a warm, flickering glow.

There was a low hum of chatter, though each group kept mostly to itself.

"We should still celebrate the holiday tomorrow," Nola's mother said. "I propose we do presents in the morning, like usual, and have a nice big brunch afterward."

"I'll turn the generator back on for a few hours tomorrow morning," Anna chimed in, having overheard them. "There will be hot chocolate and coffee, along with the rest of the muffins for anyone who wants to partake."

"Do you think the police will be able to get up here by tomorrow?" Ashley asked Anna, her expression hopeful.

"It depends on how busy the plows are," Anna told her. "I'm sure the municipal plows are going to be busy clearing the town roads, but there are plenty of people who own their own plows, and the police might be able to get them to help clear the mountain roads. Given the circumstances, I imagine we will be a priority."

They fell silent for a moment out of respect for the dead. Across the room, Nola heard Hailey sigh as she leaned back against Anthony's shoulder.

"This would be the perfect romantic getaway, if it wasn't for what happened to that poor man," she said.

"We should have a winter wedding, Anthony. This is so cozy. I just adore the atmosphere."

"Hold on," Ashley spoke up, her voice sharp. Hailey jolted, apparently not having realized everyone else had fallen silent. "I thought you two were already married."

Hailey set up quickly and Anthony stiffened where he sat. "Did we say that?" he asked. "You must have misheard us."

"No, my sister is right," Nola said, crossing her arms. "You introduced yourselves as Hailey and Anthony Smith, but I'm starting to think you were both lying about that. I accidentally saw your ID when I found your wallet today, Anthony, and it had your last name as Anderson."

"You gave fake names?" Mrs. Russell asked, her gaze suddenly sharpening. "I don't like this at all. There was a murder, and now we have two people who can't keep their stories straight?"

Hailey bit her lip, worry twisting her features. Anthony looked like he was about to say something, but she suddenly burst out, "We lied, okay? I swear, neither of us had anything to do with Frank. I… I'm married, but my marriage is failing. I've been seeing Anthony for years now, and we're planning on coming clean about our relationship soon, but I'm just not ready yet. We put down fake last names in case my husband was suspicious about my supposed business trip and called around."

"So that's who you were talking to on the phone last night," Nola said. "Your husband?"

Hailey flushed. "I *knew* you overheard that. Look, judge me all you want, but believe me when I say that we had absolutely nothing to do with Frank. We wanted to keep our affair a secret, but not so bad we'd hurt anyone over it."

"Other than your husband, of course," Mrs. Russell sniped.

Hailey flushed. Before the argument could devolve, Anna clapped her hands together, startling all of them.

"I think that's enough for tonight," she said. "Everyone should return to their cabins. I'm shutting off the generator and locking up for the night. Tomorrow is Christmas; let's all try to keep that in mind."

CHAPTER ELEVEN

Christmas morning dawned bright and sunny. When Nola pulled the curtains back, the snow outside was almost blinding. Henry, just as infected with the holiday cheer as she was, came up behind her and wrapped his arms around her waist. "Merry Christmas," he murmured into her ear.

She turned to kiss him. "Merry Christmas."

Putting their coats and boots on over their pajamas, they heaved their bag of presents next door to her parents' cabin. Ashley was already up, stacking the gifts into a pile by the fireplace. Her mother was heating up some milk for hot cocoa in a pot over the fire, and her father was fiddling with his walkie-talkie.

"Oh, did you try calling us?" she asked as Henry hung their coats up. "I think our walkie-talkie died. I sort of forgot about it."

"No, I'm trying to get some Christmas carols playing. The walkie-talkies have an AM/FM radio built in. I'm not sure what stations they get up here, though."

He got it working just as her mother started handing out mugs of hot chocolate, and they started their Christmas morning by listening to the last half of a Christmas carol while sipping the warm drinks.

When the song ended, an announcer came on. *"Merry Christmas, ladies and gentlemen. We'll get back to our normal broadcast soon, but first I have a special announcement. The authorities are still hunting for the individual suspected to be behind the theft of nearly a quarter of a million dollars from an armored car during the first night of that nasty storm that hit the region this holiday season. The vehicle the suspect was driving is a midsized, silver SUV, and the driver was wearing a dark blue coat. If you spot this individual, or happen to know someone who came into a suspiciously large amount of cash recently, please call the following number…"*

He rattled off the number while Nola stared at the walkie-talkie, frowning. The description of the SUV sounded familiar – wasn't that what Victoria's vehicle looked like? And she had a dark blue coat…

She shook her head, refocusing on the drink. There was no way Victoria was behind the theft. Although… she had been in the area when it happened, hadn't she? She remembered hearing about the theft on the radio while they were driving up here, and Victoria had already been at the resort when they got there. She would have had time to flee the scene and hide out in her cabin before the report hit the air.

"Everything all right?" Henry murmured to her. She looked up and nodded, forcing herself to focus on the holiday for now.

They opened their gifts after they finished their cocoa, and for a brief span of time, it felt just like any other Christmas. After the gifts were done, they decided to head over to the lobby building as a family.

Nola wasn't disappointed. Anna had plugged in the lights for the big Christmas tree in the corner, and there was a table laden with muffins, coffee, and hot chocolate. A radio played Christmas music much more clearly than the little walkie-talkie did. Victoria was there, surprisingly; she was sitting in an armchair by the fire, eating a blueberry muffin and sipping a cup of coffee, her winter coat still on. Nola stared at it. Yep, definitely dark blue.

Henry nudged her, raising his eyebrows. She bit her lip, then nodded toward the Christmas tree. They walked over to it, and she pretended to admire it while she explained her suspicions to him in whispers.

"I know it's probably a coincidence," she admitted. "There's no way Victoria is the one who stole all that money from the armored car, right?"

"Maybe there's something to it," Henry said slowly, deep in thought. "*Someone* killed Frank. We know that for a fact. Maybe I'm wrong, but none of the people we went ice skating with yesterday strike me as the type to stab a man to death."

"Does Victoria?"

He shrugged. "It's hard to say. She's the only one who didn't join us, after all. None of us have had a chance to get a feel for her."

Nola frowned. "She wouldn't let us help her with her bags," she remembered. "She was reluctant to leave them in her vehicle when we went to the lobby to look for a shovel. And she was ready to drive off, even though it was dangerous. Maybe she's worried someone's going to steal the money if she leaves her bags unsupervised."

"We should probably leave it for the police," he said in a low voice. "We can tell them what we suspect, and they'll handle it."

"I guess. And maybe I'm wrong. She's here now, after all." She looked at the other woman, who seemed content to slowly make her way through the muffin and coffee. Nola frowned. "She would have had plenty of time to hide the money while we were all at the lake yesterday. What if she hid it somewhere, and is planning on coming back for it after the search for the money and the hubbub surrounding Frank's death dies down?"

"I'm not saying I don't believe you, I just don't see how we can be sure," he said quietly. "You've always had good intuition, but that's not going to be enough right now."

She hesitated. What she was about to suggest was going to sound completely crazy, but she had to know. It was never going to stop bothering her if she didn't at least try to find out the truth.

"She's here now," she pointed out. "Which means her cabin is empty. We could… go snoop through it."

Henry hesitated, but after holding her gaze for a moment, he seemed to realize how important this was to her. She fell in love with him just a little more as he nodded and nodded toward the door.

They managed to sneak out of the building on the pretense that they wanted to grab a charger and charge their phones while the power was on. Mrs. Russell waved as she walked by them in the parking lot. Nola waved back, and as soon as the older woman stepped through the doors into the lobby, she and Henry turned toward the last cabin in the row. Victoria's cabin. She was disappointed to see that the curtains were all pulled shut when they reached it. Of course they were. What had she expected?

She turned, surveying the parking lot. No one else was outside. Victoria's SUV was freshly cleaned off of snow, sparkling merrily in the sunlight. Silver, just like she had thought.

"Hey, Henry," she said. "Do you have the key to our cabin?"

He took it out of his pocket. "Right here. Why?"

"I want to try something."

She took it from him and slipped it into the lock. It fit easily, and when she turned the key, the deadbolt slid open. They exchanged a look.

"Shoddy security," Henry muttered.

She was a little surprised that it had worked, but not truly shocked. She remembered changing out the doorknobs at their house when they first bought it, and how the pack of four new doorknobs had come with matching keys. It was easier, since one key unlocked them all, if less secure.

They stepped into the cabin together. Nola shut the door behind her but didn't lock it. She slipped the key into her pocket and looked around. The cabin had been tidied up compared to what she saw yesterday. The duffel bag was sitting empty in the kitchen table, but a suitcase was lying on the couch, still packed, with the top lying open. She walked over to it and peered inside, but all she saw was a mountain of clothes.

"I don't feel right doing this," Henry admitted. "If we're wrong, we're invading her privacy for no reason."

"Maybe you're right." She sighed, her eyes landing on the empty duffel bag. Had she let the strange thrill of solving a mystery get the better of her? Then her eyes narrowed. The *empty* duffel bag. "Hold on. Where did she put whatever was in her duffel bag? Remember how heavy it looked the other night?"

I don't know," he said. "Maybe she had towels or bedding in it. Not everyone likes using the provided linens when they stay somewhere."

Grumbling to herself, she wandered into the attached kitchen, slowly coming to terms with the fact that they probably weren't going to find anything. Her eyes ghosted past the dish drying rack, then snapped back to it. There were a handful of dishes inside, but the one that stood out was a black-handled kitchen knife. A knife block to the left of the stove was filled with wood-handled knives, which told her this knife didn't fit with the rest of the cabin's cutlery.

But the kitchen in the main building had black-handled knives. She had helped wash them after everyone cooked dinner together the night before.

"Henry –" she started, but before she could point the knife out to him, Victoria pulled the cabin's door open and paused, her gaze flitting between them.

"What in the *world* are the two of you doing here?"

CHAPTER TWELVE

Nola froze. Henry stepped closer to her, and she took some meager comfort in his protective height beside her. Victoria looked pale, but her voice was livid.

"Why are you in my cabin? You have no right to be in here."

"I'm sorry –" Nola started, but the other woman stepped forward, every step stiff and laced with anger.

"Get out, right now."

Henry touched her elbow to encourage her to move, and they started toward the door, but Nola paused, looking back at the kitchen knife in the dish rack. Henry paused too, finally seeing it, judging by the sudden frown on his face.

Still angry, Victoria grabbed his arm and yanked him toward the door, making him stumble. "What are you doing? Get out!"

Nola felt a hot wave of anger flash through her.

"Hey, keep your hands off him," she snapped, grabbing Victoria's poofy coat sleeve and pulling her back. It wasn't a hard pull – she wasn't trying to hurt the other woman, she just wanted her to get her hands off of Henry. But there was a ripping sound, and the sleeve of Victoria's coat tore off.

The three of them stood, stunned for a moment, as the sleeve fell to the floor. Nola's mouth worked, and she remembered seeing the sleeve ripped off of the coat the day before, when she got a glance into Victoria's cabin. It made sense that a patchwork sewing job might not have been very tough, but how had her sleeve gotten ripped off in the first place?

Snapping out of it, Victoria ducked down and grabbed the sleeve, backing away from the two of them. Nola's eyes tracked the ragged hem of the coat's shoulder, and she saw something green and papery poking out of it. Her breath caught in her throat. Victoria's eyes followed her gaze and she tensed, a flurry of emotions crossing her face. Anger, fear… resignation.

The green paper was money. Her coat was stuffed full of cash. Nola took a step back, dizzy with the revelation.

"You… you *are* the one who robbed that armored car," she managed weakly. "You sewed all the money into your coat?"

Despite herself, she was a little impressed. A coat stuffed full of money was much less noticeable than a bulky duffel bag. She wouldn't be surprised if the woman had hidden the cash in more places as well; maybe in the seats of her SUV or the lining of her suitcase. Somehow, she had efficiently made almost a quarter of a million dollars vanish.

Victoria stared at them for a horrified second. A hundred-dollar bill slipped out of the shoulder of her ripped coat and fluttered to the floor.

"Did you kill Frank too?" Nola asked, her voice cracking. She felt Henry's hand on her shoulder, and she knew he wanted to leave. But she had to know.

"Hold on," Victoria said, her words frantic and rapid. "I'll… I'll split it with you. It's a lot of money. Life-changing. All you have to do is not tell anyone. I shouldn't… I shouldn't have done what I did to Frank. The report about the theft came on over the radio while I was checking in. He saw my SUV, saw me, and put two and two together. I denied everything when he accused me, of course, but I could tell he didn't believe me."

"And somehow that led to you stabbing him to death in a laundry room?" Henry asked, aghast. She could feel his tension through the grip on her shoulder.

"A buzzer went off," Victoria said. "He told me to sit tight while he unloaded the dryer, and he'd bring out some nice warm towels for me, but my gut told me he was going to call the police. I… I found a knife in the kitchen, and I confronted him in the laundry room. You don't understand how much money this is. It's going to change our lives, even if we split it between the three of us. I don't want to hurt anyone else. I just want to get out of here, go home, and put all of this behind me."

"I'm still confused. Are you some sort of professional thief?" Nola asked, shaken by the confession. "Who just… robs an armored truck?"

"I wasn't planning on it," Victoria said quickly. "The weather was bad, and the driver went off the road. I think I was probably the first person to drive by the wreck. I stopped to see if I could help, but the driver was already dead. And the truck's frame was all twisted; the door to the back had popped off. I realized what was in the bags in the back, and I could hardly believe it. It was all just sitting there, free to grab, you know? I never meant for things to gets out of hand. Please, just take the money and don't say anything. I can't go back in time and undo what happened to Frank, but the three of us can still benefit from this."

"No way," Nola said. "You're asking us to keep quiet about *murder*."

"I don't think either of us would be able to enjoy that money knowing two people died for it," Henry added.

"Please, just take it," Victoria begged. She glanced back toward the kitchen, where the knives were, and Nola wondered if she was trying to judge the likelihood of overpowering and silencing them both.

In the end, she never had to find out. Someone knocked on the door and then pulled it open without waiting for a response. Anna peeked inside, her expression bright. "The snowplows are coming up the road. I'm getting everyone together to—"

Breaking off midsentence, she froze, looking between Nola, Henry, and Victoria, then down to Victoria's sleeve, as another hundred-dollar bill fluttered out and fell slowly to the floor.

Victoria seemed to realize there was no getting out of this. She slumped into a kitchen chair, lowering her head to her hands with a moan of despair.

With the snowplows on their way, the police wouldn't be far behind. All of a sudden, Nola felt lighter. It was Christmas Day. The snowy forest was breathtaking, all of her loved ones were together and safe, and not one but two crimes had been solved.

This was one unforgettable holiday.

Printed in Great Britain
by Amazon